The Summer Kid

by
Myrna Neuringer Levy

Illustrations by
Alice Priestley

SECOND STORY Press

FEMINIST PUBLISHERS

CANADIAN CATALOGUING IN PUBLICATION DATA

Levy, Myrna Neuringer
The summer kid
ISBN 0-929005-20-1

I. Learning disabled child – Juvenile fiction.
1. Title.

PS8573.E99S8 1991   jC813'.54   C91-093464-9
PZ7.L499Su 1991

*Second Story Press gratefully acknowledges the assistance of the
Ontario Arts Council and the Canada Council*

Printed and bound in Canada

Published by
SECOND STORY PRESS
760 Bathurst Street
Toronto Canada M5S 2R6

Dedicated to D.H.N. and E.J.L.
because they always said
'Yes, you can'

1

"OUCH!" A needle of pain shot through Karen's toe. "What are all these stones doing on the dock?"

She crouched down, one hand over her wounded toe. With the other hand she began to pick up the smaller stones and toss them into the water.

"Hey, that's my fort! You break it!"

Karen turned her head to see a small, skinny boy, carrying an armload of muddy stones. They looked at each other.

"I didn't know this was a fort." Karen rubbed her toe where the bruise was beginning to spread. "But I just hurt myself on one of your stones. They're dangerous. And in any case they shouldn't be here blocking traffic."

"Traffic? There are no cars here."

Karen was in no mood for smart alec remarks. "I don't find it funny," she said. The needle of pain was now flashing up to her ankle.

The little boy didn't answer. He had dropped his stones onto the dock, and now began to arrange them carefully.

"Look, you can't just build your fort across the dock. People have to walk here." Annoyance rose in Karen at this strange little kid who, unasked, was taking over her grandmother's dock.

"I just build a fort." He continued to place his stones in a neat row.

Karen made an effort to hold her temper. "You can build a fort," she said. "Just don't take up the whole dock. Here, let me show you." She dropped to her knees and began to shift some of the stones.

"Oh, a square." He began to help. "Right," said Karen. "You can make a smaller square on this side of the dock. Then people can still walk down the other side." She sat back on her heels and watched him work.

He was the same height as her brother, but where six-year-old Michael was round ("Butter-ball" Dad teased; "Just baby fat" Mom would retort), this little boy was thin, with stick-like arms.

Oh, crumb-bum, Karen thought. As if things weren't already off to a bad start. To begin with, Michael had broken his ankle which meant no family vacation this year. Karen had always looked forward to the annual two-week holiday at the cottage next to Grandma's, and her heart fell into her running shoes when she heard Mom tell Grandma that they wouldn't be coming.

But then Grandma invited Karen to come up by herself. What a great idea! A vacation on her own! Ever since Michael was born, Karen had to share everything. She had to share Mom and Dad with Michael; she had to share her toys; at school she even had to share ideas with her Grade Four classmates.

How wonderful to have two whole weeks alone at the cottage! To swim whenever she wanted, for as long as she wanted. And Grandma would be sure to make Karen's favourite meals, take her to the Historical Museum to see the doll collection, maybe take her across the lake to play with the Campbell sisters. When Grandpa came up on weekends he and Karen could work on crossword puzzles together.

She wouldn't have to share anything with anyone, unless she wanted to.

Then Grandma rented the cottage next door to an unknown lady with a little boy. At first Karen didn't think this would be a problem. But then last night Grandma had said she hoped Karen would get along nicely with the little boy.

"But Grandma," Karen had groaned. "I can't play with a little boy!"

"Why not?" Grandma had wanted to know. "You play with your brother, don't you?"

"Grandma, that's the only reason I play with him. Do you think I'd ever play with Michael if he weren't my brother? If you had to rent the cottage, why couldn't you rent it to someone with a girl my age?"

Grandma had told Karen to lower her voice. "You know how voices carry near water. I don't want Dawn Jones to hear us arguing."

Karen let out a long sigh.

A woman's voice interrupted her thoughts.

"Tommy? Tommy, where are you?" The voice was sharp with worry.

The little boy dropped his stone and stood up as suddenly as if pulled by a string. His head turned in the direction of the voice.

"There you are." A young woman wrapped in a bathrobe came hurrying down to the dock. "What did Mommy tell you about going near the water?"

"Don't go near the water unless Mommy is with you," the little boy recited.

"That's absolutely right." The young woman was firm. "I just wanted you to wait a few minutes until I got dressed and then I was going to walk down here with you."

"I sorry." Tommy hung his head. Then suddenly he began to jump and shout. "I builded a fort, a big one! Over here!"

"A fort? Good. Let me see."

The young woman put a foot on the dock, and then she saw Karen. "Oh, hello! You must be Mrs. Burton's granddaughter."

Karen nodded.

"She told me that you were coming up here yesterday – I'm Dawn Jones. And I suppose you met my son, Tommy."

Karen nodded again.

"We're renting the cottage next to your grand-mother's. We were so lucky to find it available at the last minute! And Tommy is so happy to have someone to play with. He just loves to... "

But before she could finish, Tommy had pulled her onto the dock.

"Come see my fort, Mommy."

Dawn leaned over to inspect the pile of stones. "Very nice, Tommy. You always build such good forts."

"I was just explaining to your little boy that he can't build his fort across the dock. It's dangerous. I stubbed my toe on his stones this morning," explained Karen sweetly.

"Oh, of course," agreed Dawn, "I'm so sorry. Is your toe all right?" And she took Tommy by the hand. "Remember, Tommy, baby, we're guests here. This place belongs to Mrs. Burton and you have to behave."

"No Tommy baby! I am Thomas," he insisted.

"Right, Tommy: I keep forgetting." Dawn straightened, letting go of Tommy's hand. "That's a good fort, but it needs a doorway. Are you going to make a doorway?" Sounding more cheerful with the change of subject, she turned to Karen. "Are you going to be here a little while?"

Karen nodded.

"Then would you mind looking after Tommy for a few minutes? I just want to go up to the cottage to get dressed."

"Well, all right." Karen couldn't keep the reluctance out of her voice. "At home I always have to watch my brother, Michael."

"Yes, your brother – your Grandmother told me what happened to him. Poor little boy. Well, I'll be as fast as I can." And she hurried up the path.

"Double crumb-bum," said Karen. She picked up a stone and turned it over in her hand. Was she going to end up babysitting for her whole vacation? Why bother having a vacation at all? For a moment Karen felt like taking the bus back to the city.

Tommy had finished building his fort, a square with a small opening. On either side of the entrance he'd balanced several stones to form gateposts. Now he stood looking at Karen.

"Say, Tommy, want to play a game?"

Tommy shrugged his shoulders. "Don't know any games."

"Don't worry, I know lots of games. Have you ever skipped stones into the water?"

"Skip? I can skip."

He ran off the dock and began to skip along the path, chanting. "An' one foot an' the other foot, an' one foot an' the other foot...." He turned to look at Karen. "My teacher learned me to skip this year."

"Taught me," corrected Karen.

"No, she taught *me*."

"Right. Some holiday this is turning out to be," muttered Karen under her breath. "Look, Tommy," she said out loud, "that's not the kind of skipping I meant. Skipping stones means throwing stones across the water. Here – let me show you."

With a twist of her arm she threw the stone out over the lake, so that it skidded along the surface of the water before it sank.

"I can do that!" Tommy picked up a pebble and threw it into the water. A small spurt of water flashed where the pebble had disappeared.

"You see that splash? I make a big splash."

"You sure did," agreed Karen. She remembered

how difficult it had been to teach Michael to skip stones last summer. "Tell you what, how about a contest to see who can throw the pebble the farthest into the lake?"

"I can throw it acrost the lake!"

"Doubt it. This lake is two kilometres wide. You'll be pretty good if you can throw a pebble as far as the end of the dock."

They spent the next little while taking turns. At first Karen's stones went farther than Tommy's, but then he began to catch up. Karen's experience with Michael had taught her to occasionally throw short, so that Tommy could win a round or two. She showed him how to bring his arm way back and throw with a smooth motion. After a few tries, his pebbles did go a bit further and he was delighted.

When Dawn came down to the dock Tommy proudly showed her how far he could throw his stones.

"That's very good, Tommy. Here, let me put your hat on. The sun's getting hot."

She placed a Blue Jays' baseball cap on Tommy's head. It was much too large for him, and floated awkwardly over the tops of his ears. Karen thought he looked ridiculous, but instead of teasing him she tried to make conversation.

"I see you're a Blue Jays fan," said Karen. "My Dad took me to a game at the SkyDome last week. The roof was open, and the Jays won. Have you noticed that the Jays always win when the roof is open?"

Tommy was silent, his face blank. Perhaps he hadn't heard her.

Karen tried again. "Well, why do you think the Jays always win when the SkyDome roof is open?"

Dawn opened, then closed her mouth. She seemed to be having an argument with herself. Tommy remained wordless.

Finally Dawn broke the silence, handing him a small yellow plastic pail and shovel. "Here," she said, "I thought you might like to play on the beach."

Tommy nodded. Then he turned to Karen and said, slowly and clearly, "Roofs don't open." He carried his pail over to the beach, set it down and began to dig in the wet sand. "I make a mud fort now," he announced.

Karen was surprised. Tommy's answer didn't make sense. Surely everyone who lived in Toronto knew about the SkyDome and its retractable roof. But she let it go. Now would be a perfect moment to make her escape.

"I have to help my grandmother," she told Dawn, and limped up the path to the cottage.

In her bedroom Karen found the bag of books she'd checked out of the library before leaving Toronto, including the new Jean Little book the librarian had saved for her. Maybe I'll just sit in the hammock and read, she decided.

A soft breeze rocked the hammock, but Karen couldn't seem to concentrate. Her toe throbbed, for one thing, and as she fingered the pale blue bruise her thoughts returned to Tommy Jones. What a strange little kid! Some of the things he said made no sense at all. That is, when he had anything to say – most of the time he didn't even speak. Not like the six-year-olds I know, she thought, remembering her chatterbox brother and his crazy friends.

Karen sat with her book open to the first page for a long time.

2

KAREN DIDN'T SEE Tommy or his mother for the rest of the day. After lunch she went into town with her grandmother. They did a few errands, toured the main street and treated themselves to an ice cream at the Dairy Dell. There was no sign of Tommy or his mother when Karen went down to the dock for a late afternoon swim.

But for the rest of the week she wasn't so lucky. Every time she went down to the beach there he was. When Karen wanted to take a running dive off the dock she had to wait until Tommy slowly dogpaddled out of her way. And whenever she wanted to sit on the dock and read, she had to step over Tommy, always building another of his endless forts. Piles of stones and more piles of stones, just where Karen wanted to sunbathe.

But at least Dawn didn't ask her to babysit again. In fact, Dawn never seemed to leave Tommy's side. And Tommy didn't say a lot. He was usually building or digging in the sand.

Maybe, he doesn't want to play with me, thought Karen, any more than I want to play with him. He'd probably be happier if Michael were here – a boy his own age. Except that Michael didn't have the patience for building things.

Then one day Grandma and Karen were hanging up their swimsuits behind the cottage just as Dawn was parking her car. She and Tommy came over as Grandma was passing the clothespegs to Karen.

"Well, Tommy, where were you this morning?" asked Grandma.

Tommy was silent.

"Go on," prompted Dawn, "tell Mrs. Burton where we went today."

"Well, um," Tommy began, "we went ... we see the boats go in the big bathtub, and then the evulator takes them up to the next lake."

Grandma looked puzzled. Karen, too, at first, but then she said, "Oh, I got it, you went to see the boats in the lift locks between the lakes."

Tommy nodded.

Turning to Dawn, Karen said, "Your little boy has a cute way of describing things."

Dawn hesitated for a few seconds before answering. "Actually, Tommy isn't that little."

"What do you mean?" Karen was curious.

Dawn paused again. Then she spoke as if she had to think about every word.

"I mean that although Tommy may be small, he is not really a little boy. People can be measured in different ways, not only by their size."

She took Tommy's hand. "Come on, let's make some lunch."

Karen watched them walk to their cottage. What did Dawn mean, that Tommy was not really a little boy? So what was he really? A chipmunk? And what was this stuff about measuring people in different ways? There's something going on, thought Karen, and it smells like a secret.

Over lunch Karen put her thoughts into words. "You know, Grandma, there's something strange about Tommy."

"What do you mean 'strange'?"

"Oh, I don't know. He's so quiet. Sometimes when you ask him a question he just sits and stares into space before he answers."

"Well, not everyone is a chatterbox like you."

"And then he doesn't understand so many things you say."

"Like what?"

"Like expressions. The first day on the dock when I told him he was blocking traffic, he thought I meant real cars. And look at the way he described the lift locks."

"Well, maybe he's a literal kid."

"What's a literal kid?"

"See, you don't know everything either! A literal person takes the meaning of words as they are, not as expressions that could mean something different."

"And his mother is always worrying about him. She's so overprotective," continued Karen.

"That's understandable. Tommy's never been to a cottage by a lake before. She just wants to make sure he's safe," said Grandma. "But tell you what. I haven't been paying much attention to Tommy. Maybe I'll take a closer look."

"Sure." Karen returned to her plate of steaming macaroni. She knew there was something different about Tommy, even if she couldn't say what it was.

3

OVER BREAKFAST, Grandma remarked that it looked like a cloudy day. "Perfect for picking blueberries on Blueberry Hill," she suggested. "Then we can bake our pies this afternoon for the barbecue on Sunday."

"Great!" agreed Karen. "I'll get dressed and make my bed in two seconds."

"Make it three and do a good job," countered Grandma.

But then Grandma said something that punctured Karen's excitement as quickly as a pin bursts a balloon. "I think I'll ask Dawn and Tommy to join us. They'll be glad of an outing on a day like today, and we could certainly use some help."

Karen rolled her eyes. "Oh no! Sure, we can use some help," she said. "But not their kind of help; if

Tommy is anything like Michael he'll eat more than he picks. And then he'll get bored in ten minutes, and he'll just run around the bushes, and I'll be the one to chase after him."

"Now, Karen," said Grandma firmly. "Tommy Jones seems like a quiet little boy. I'm sure he's a very nice child."

'Nice' was Grandma's favourite word when describing children. Nice children were polite, played quietly, and certainly never talked back to adults. So Karen didn't say anything, but she rolled her eyes again.

Half an hour later Karen found her grandmother outside the toolshed in conversation with Dawn. Tommy's baseball cap had slipped down over his ears and he was gripping the handle of his yellow plastic pail between small fingers.

"Thank you so much for including us, Mrs. Burton," Dawn was saying as Grandma handed her a wooden fruit basket. "This will be a very good experience for Tommy, I'm sure. He's never picked blueberries before."

"I pick apples at my school," Tommy told everyone. "A wagon take us to the trees." He looked around. "A wagon take us to the blue-berries?"

"No, Tommy," said Grandma, laughing. "We can walk to Blueberry Hill. It's not far at all. And now that everyone's ready, we're off!"

They began walking along the road that ran behind the cottages. After a few minutes they left the lake behind them and followed the old dirt track, deeply rutted, that led up the hill to a neighbouring farm.

Karen stopped several times to enjoy the clouds. The sky was a giant stage and the clouds were dancers in grey costumes, moving to the music of the wind in the trees. When we get back from Blueberry Hill, Karen promised herself, I'll go down to the dock and lie on my back to watch the clouds.

"Oh, look! Pretty flowers!" Tommy pointed to the bright yellow buttercups growing near the fence.

"Don't touch anything, Tommy." A note of alarm had entered Dawn's voice. "There could be poison ivy in there."

"I wouldn't worry about it, Dawn," said

Grandma easily. "In all the years I've been coming up here I've never seen or heard of a case of poison ivy."

"Thanks," said Dawn, with a quick glance at Grandma. But then she added, "Still, Tommy, I don't want you wandering away from us. You might get lost."

"I be good."

Karen took Tommy by the hand and drew him over to the yellow flowers. "Look, Tommy, these are buttercups."

"Cutter bups?"

"No, bu-tter-cups," Karen repeated slowly.

"Butter flowers? You eat them?"

"No, silly," said Karen; and then she made an effort to be patient. "They're probably called buttercups because they're yellow, and shaped like cups."

"Oh." Tommy nodded. Then something else caught his attention. "See? A butterfly. Go, butterfly! Eat buttercup!" And he laughed at his own joke.

At the top of the hill they found the blueberry bushes, all together in a clump. So many birds were chattering in the branches that it seemed as if the bushes must be alive. Then the birds sensed their approach and swooped up into the air, alighting in a nearby stand of trees.

"Oh, Grandma, we interrupted their breakfast," exclaimed Karen.

"Don't worry, my sweet, there are berries enough for everyone." Grandma put down her basket. "Why don't you and Tommy start on this one," she suggested, "and Dawn and I will tackle the big bushes over here. Try not to let Tommy eat too many berries."

"You don't have to worry about that," said Dawn quickly. "Tommy won't eat blueberries."

"Why not?" asked Grandma.

Dawn looked embarrassed. "Tommy won't eat any foods that are blue," she admitted in a low voice.

"So nothing blue will do?" Grandma shook her head, amused. "Don't kids have the strangest eating habits?"

"Then you've heard of this before?"

"Of course I have," said Grandma, looking straight at Karen. "I have a lovely granddaughter who won't eat fish when it looks like a fish. She'll only eat fish when it comes out of a can. And my grandson, Michael, is so crazy about ice cream that he wants it on his breakfast cereal instead of milk."

Dawn smiled. "This blue food business started two years ago," she explained, still in a low voice. "We were out for dinner with friends and the dessert was blueberry pie. The other little boy began to tease Tommy when his teeth turned blue, and Tommy got very upset. Since then he won't eat anything blue or purple. No grapes, or grape jelly, or grape juice."

She dropped a handful of ripe berries into her basket. "But the doctor says there's nothing wrong if Tommy won't eat blue foods. He says most children grow out of food fads."

"I expect he's right," said Grandma.

While Grandma and Dawn compared notes on the eating habits of children, Karen had been showing Tommy how to pick blueberries. "Just the dark blue ones – leave the green ones to ripen," she told him. She made sure he knew how to pluck the berries off their tiny stems. "If you pick the stems and the leaves with the berries we'll only have to clean them later," she pointed out.

To her surprise, Tommy followed instructions to the letter, placing the berries one by one in his little yellow pail. "You see, Karen, I'm not squooshing them."

How different from Michael, Karen was forced to admit. Last summer five-year-old Michael had grabbed berries by the fistful, dropping stems, leaves, and crushed berries together in the basket. By lunchtime he'd been so sticky with berry juice that Karen's mother had to run a bath. Tommy was certainly easier to take care of, Karen thought, but so quiet that she was almost uncomfortable. She glanced at him as he worked alongside her, softly singing a wordless little tune. An unexpected pang of longing for her noisy brother suddenly rose up in Karen.

Dawn was also frequently glancing over at Tommy, as if to reassure herself. Then she began a new subject.

"Tell me, Mrs. Burton, when are these pies going to get eaten?"

"On Sunday. Every year around this time we have a ball game and a big barbecue to give the

townspeople and the cottagers a chance to get together. We all have a great time! There's a baseball game at the local school – the All-Year All-Stars play the Summer Kids. Then we troop over to the Coopers for a potluck barbecue. You and Tommy must join us."

"Oh, Mrs. Burton," protested Dawn, "I'm just renting the cottage for two weeks. We're not regular summer people."

"Doesn't matter! Lots of people are renting cottages these days. Whoever happens to be here on the day of the barbecue comes along, and this year that includes you. Besides, you and Tommy are helping me pick blueberries for the pies, so it's only fair that you have a chance to eat them." And she gave Dawn one of her 'that-settles-it' looks.

"All right. We'd love to come. But Tommy's not very good at baseball."

"Don't worry. None of the summer kids play very well. The whole idea is to have fun."

"But baking all these berries into pies must be a lot of work," Dawn continued. "Perhaps you'll let me come to your cottage this afternoon and give you a hand."

"Well, I'd certainly be glad of your company."
Grandma looked pleased. "But it's not as much
work as it used to be because" – and she dropped
her voice to a whisper and looked around in all
directions – "because I cheat!"

A large black crow chose that very moment to
soar across the sky, screeching "Caw, caw, caw!"

"Shhh!" Grandma advised the crow. "There's
no need to tell the whole world." She shook her
basket of berries lightly, to help them settle. "Not
that it's such a terrible thing."

"Grandma, how do you cheat?" Karen's curios-
ity had pulled her into the conversation.

"I use frozen piecrusts, if you must know." It
had been taking too much time making the
piecrusts herself, Grandma went on to explain. So
now she bought frozen piecrusts and filled them
with blueberries mixed with sugar for delicious
pies. "It says right on the package," said Grandma
innocently, "that you can bake pies just like
Grandma used to make."

Dawn began to laugh, then Karen. All three
were laughing so hard they had to hold their
sides when Tommy joined them. "Why are you

laughing, Mommy?"

Dawn was still whooping as she tried to answer. "Tommy boy, I'll explain it to you later," she said, wiping her eyes.

Grandma recovered first. "But Mommy will only explain," she teased Tommy, "if you promise to keep it a secret."

"What secret?"

"Don't worry about it," Dawn assured him; and to Grandma, "Look, I think Tommy must be hungry. We'll start walking back."

"No need," said Grandma, "I brought a snack for all of us. And we have to eat it up because I don't want to carry it home." Grandma pulled from her knapsack four small cartons of juice and four small bags of sandwiches. "Now we don't want to leave any litter, so give me back your garbage when you've finished," she said as she handed out the snacks.

Karen chose an evergreen whose branches grew so low that they formed an umbrella over her head, and sat down in her very own private shade. She plunged her straw into the carton and drank deeply.

Tommy also put his straw into the carton and drank. Then he unwrapped his sandwich. Grandma's sandwiches were peanut butter with grape jelly, always a favourite with Karen and Michael. But not with Tommy.

Karen watched in amazement as Tommy lifted the top slice of bread and, using his plastic bag as a towel, carefully wiped off the grape jelly. Then he bit cautiously into the remains of his sandwich.

Weirder and weirder, decided Karen. Tommy Jones is one weird boy. Michael would have eaten that whole sandwich by now. And she began to wonder what Michael might be eating for lunch, back in the city.

Grandma held her hand up to the sky. "Did I feel a drop of rain? I think we'd better walk back before the sky opens."

"The sky opens?" asked Tommy.

"No, of course not. That's just an expression," answered Grandma. "But we should get going. Karen, don't swing your basket like that, you'll spill all your berries. Remember last time!"

"Don't remind me," Karen muttered. Last summer on the walk home she and Michael had pretended they were soldiers marching in a parade. Shoulders back, arms swinging, faster and faster, giggling – and then their baskets suddenly crashed together scattering blueberries across the path. What a disaster! This year Karen took care not to swing her basket.

A fine drizzle had begun to fall from the now-darkened sky.

"Come on, Tommy, shake a leg. You're getting wet." Grandma quickened her steps.

Tommy stopped walking. He looked down at his legs, then at Grandma. "Shake a leg, not get wet?"

"No, Tommy. That's not what Mrs. Burton meant," explained Dawn. "Shake a leg means to walk faster. Let's do that. "

"Tell you what," said Grandma as they neared Dawn's cottage. "We'll all go home and have lunch, and maybe a nap. Then, if it's still raining, you and Tommy come over for a visit. The kids can play together while you and I bake pies."

"That's a lovely idea," agreed Dawn. "You're very kind. I'm sure Tommy will enjoy playing with Karen."

Karen wanted to scream at the top of her lungs. She wanted to shout: Doesn't anyone care what *I* want to do? Maybe *I* don't want to play with Tommy!

But she knew before she drew the next breath that if she "displayed her temper," to use Grandma's phrase, Grandma would be deeply upset. And it wasn't Grandma's fault that Mom, Dad, and Michael were back in the city and Karen up here at the cottage by herself. By herself, that is, except for the weird little kid next door.

So she shrugged a what-do-I-care shrug. Then she walked faster, to get out in front of the others.

4

LUNCH WAS OVER and it was still raining heavily when Dawn and Tommy appeared at the door. Dawn held a jacket over her head, and Tommy had changed his baseball cap for a shiny red rainhat. In they came, stamping their feet to shake off the rain.

Grandma showed Dawn the counter where the washed berries were waiting in huge bowls. Dawn tied an apron around her waist and began to help separate the frozen piecrusts.

Karen led Tommy to the screened porch at the back of the cottage. "Well, Tommy, what would you like to do?"

Tommy stood in the middle of the room. He seemed smaller without his hat. "I dunno," he said, looking around for ideas. The porch was a comfortable place, somehow even cozier with the rain drumming against the roof. The couches and chairs were covered with brightly flowered prints, and two bookcases that flanked the doorway into the cottage were crammed with books and magazines.

"Say – I know." Karen's eyes lit up. "We can play school. I'll be the teacher and you can be my class."

"I dunno."

"Well, I won't give you real work, like math or a project. Maybe you'd like to draw a picture." She reached into a bookcase and pulled out a pad of paper and a box of old broken crayons.

"A picture? I draw a picture." Tommy flipped the pad open to a clean page. For the first time since Karen had met him, he looked excited.

"Great. You do that," said Karen. "You draw a picture and I'll sit here and read." She curled up on a couch under the window and went back to her book.

Some time later Karen looked up to see Tommy standing before her. Wordless, he handed her his drawing. She took a quick glance at it, expecting to see the awkward-looking figures that Michael usually drew. But what she saw made her gasp with surprise – Tommy had drawn Blueberry Hill! There were the blueberry bushes, with a flock of birds hovering above them. A small boy in a baseball cap was picking berries with one hand and holding a yellow pail in the other. Dark grey clouds filled the sky, just as they had that morning. Tommy had even drawn a clump of small yellow flowers in one corner. Beneath the buttercups, in neat cursive writing, was his name: Thomas Jones.

"This is incredible, Tommy." Karen was impressed. Tommy's drawing was easily as good as anything she or her friends might have drawn.

"This a very good drawing. You should show it to your mother."

Tommy nodded. "She'll put it on the fridgedator."

He disappeared into the kitchen. Karen heard an enthusiastic "Wonderful!" from her grandmother, and from Dawn, "Excellent. We'll have to put this on the fridge when we get home."

Karen heard Tommy ask, "I go home now, Mommy? I want to play Lego."

Evidently Dawn wasn't ready. "Oh, Tommy, I

can't leave just now. We're in the middle of a
streusel topping for the pies. Can't you find anything else to do?"

Karen didn't hear an answer from Tommy. She
made sure she was deep in her book when he came
back to the porch. He looked at the drawing pad,
then at Karen, and stood for a minute without
speaking.

Then he returned to the kitchen and tried again.
"I go home now? I want to play Lego."

"Soon, Tommy, soon." Dawn was patient but
firm.

Tommy didn't give up easily. He came back to
the porch, stood in silence for another minute, and
then repeated the whole routine. Again and again
he asked his mother if he could play with his Lego.
Dawn's answer didn't change, but her tone began
to show an edge.

Karen began a bet with herself, whether
Tommy or Dawn would give in first. She had a
hunch it would be Dawn.

But then Grandma said something that made
Karen's face burn. "Why don't we ask Karen to
take Tommy home? She won't mind – she has

nothing else to do."

Karen nearly threw her book on the floor. She couldn't shout out loud, so in her mind she shouted: I do so have something to do! And even if I didn't, I wouldn't want to do it with Tommy! Then she stuck out her tongue at Tommy's back.

Grandma called from the kitchen. "Karen, would you mind taking Tommy back to his cottage?"

"Well, I'm just in the middle of a very exciting part in my book. Can't he wait?"

"Karen," said Grandma in her 'that-settles-it' voice, "you can take your book with you. What difference does it make where you read?"

"I'm sorry to bother you," added Dawn. "I really do appreciate how helpful you've been with Tommy today."

I'll say I have, thought Karen. Slowly she picked up a book mark and placed it in her book. Then she went into the kitchen and rummaged through the cupboards to find a clean plastic bag to protect her book from the rain. Then she went to the coat rack beside the door and searched noisily through all the jackets and sweaters for her raincoat.

All the while Tommy stood by the door, waiting. Finally Karen found her old slicker. She pulled it over her head, sighed heavily, and turned to Tommy. "Well, are you ready?"

Tommy looked at his mother. "Alright, Tommy, you go back to the cottage with Karen. She'll stay with you until I'm finished here."

Karen walked beside Tommy without saying a word. The rain was gentle now. When they passed under the trees a gust of wind shook the branches, and huge drops splattered down on them. It might be kind of strange, Karen realized, to visit the cottage where she normally lived with Mom, Dad, and Michael, knowing that someone else was living in it now. Maybe that was why she felt so uncomfortable with Tommy – he was living where she used to live.

Or was it something else? Karen tried to put her finger on this feeling. It wasn't that she had anything against Tommy, she reminded herself. After all, he was just another summer kid, the way she was. Only more so – his mother was only renting the cottage this one time. By next year Karen's own family would be back at the cottage, and

Karen would never have to see Dawn Jones or her boring son again.

Maybe it's just that I prefer kids my own age, thought Karen as she followed Tommy up the steps of the cottage. And she promised herself to think about this later when she was alone. If she ever got the chance to be alone again.

5

THE SCREEN DOOR creaked as Karen opened it. Inside everything looked as it always had. But of course it would be the same, Karen told herself. The cottage was rented as furnished. Dawn and Tommy had only to bring their clothes, food, and Tommy's toys.

Karen hung up her slicker on the clothes rack behind the door. Then she helped Tommy to hang up his red rainhat.

"Okay, Tommy. You can play with your Lego now. Where is it?"

"There." Tommy pointed to the living-room floor.

"Wow." Karen had trouble believing her eyes. There on the floor was the biggest Lego layout she had ever seen. Lego cars were driving along Lego roads, up Lego ramps, and over Lego bridges. Other toy cars – some were the kind that change into robots – were parked at the base.

At the centre was a huge tower with platforms, like balconies on an apartment building. On some of the platforms, Tommy had placed cars; others held Lego people.

"This is amazing, Tommy. Fantastic! Did your mother help you set it up?"

"I love Lego."

Tommy was already sitting on the floor, beginning to construct a new tower.

To her utter amazement Karen found herself on the floor as well. She began to fiddle with some of the transformable cars. Michael had a few of these at home, but he always made a fuss if Karen went near them. "This is really great," Karen was surprised to hear herself saying. She hadn't played with Lego since Michael had taken over her set.

Tommy was driving one of his cars up a ramp. "Vroom, vroom," he murmured. Out of nowhere, an idea popped into Karen's head: the sandcastle-building contest.

When Karen had first seen the newspaper

announcement she thought it was just for little kids, or at least for families. The town council would be offering prizes for the best sandcastle built by any team of kids in a special competition at the town beach.

But as she watched Tommy's face, intent on his Lego, and remembered how successful he'd been in digging and building his forts at the dock, her idea began to come together.

What if she and Tommy entered the contest as a team? If Tommy could do anything, he could build. And Karen knew a lot about castles; she'd studied them in school. In fact last year her group had put together a castle out of papier mâché.

"Tommy, do you think you could build a castle?" she asked him.

Tommy looked up. "I dunno. I build forts."

"Right. You build forts. Could you build a fort made out of sand?"

Tommy sat very still. There was no expression on his face. It was hard to tell whether he was thinking of an answer, or if he'd even understood the question. After a while he said, "I dig sand in the park. I make sand forts."

"Well, then, that's what we're going to do. We're going to form the Burton cottage team and enter the sandcastle-building contest."

A tense look came over Tommy's face. "Team? What game we play?"

"Oh, don't worry," Karen said quickly. "You'll see what I mean when we do it. And you know what? We're going to design and practice building a castle, I mean, a fort, that's going to be the best on this lake."

Karen was too absorbed in her planning, and Tommy in his Lego, to notice when the rain stopped beating on the roof. They looked up, startled when Dawn burst through the door. "Tommy, Karen, come quick! There's a rainbow. You can see it from the edge of the dock."

"A rainbow?" Tommy didn't sound too interested.

"C'mon, Tommy!" Karen sprang to her feet and headed for the door. "You practically never see rainbows in the city." They raced down to the dock.

The sky split open. Somber grey rainclouds still filled the west, but the east was all fresh blue sky.

Falling from the clouds was a glistening rainbow.

"Oh," breathed Tommy. "I know a rainbow. I seed it on TV."

"TV is nothing like the real thing," remarked Karen.

"Take a deep breath," commanded Grandma. "Smell the fresh woods." Everyone breathed deeply. The air smelled of trees, flowers, and clover from the farm across the road. There was also a tiny whiff of something burning.

"Oh my goodness!" cried Grandma. "My pies!" They ran back to her cottage as fast as they could.

When the pies were out of the oven and cooling on the counter, Dawn said she had to do some shopping. As she and Tommy drove off, Karen offered to help Grandma clean up the kitchen. Over the dishes she told Grandma about her plan to enter the sandcastle contest.

"Oh, I'm so glad you and Tommy are getting along," Grandma smiled at Karen. "Playing together is much better than fighting."

Karen just shook her head. There wasn't any point in telling Grandma what she really thought of Tommy – that he was entirely weird. Grandma

49

didn't need to know that Karen was only including Tommy in the contest because she wanted to win. And win she certainly would – with Tommy's building skills and Karen's special knowledge of castles, the Burton team was going to put together an amazing entry.

6

THE NEXT FEW DAYS were busy.

Bright and early every morning Karen called for Tommy, and they spent several hours together on the muddy bank beside the dock. In a box of abandoned toys Karen had found her old pail and shovel. Soon Tommy could build simple three-storey structures, Karen adding the look-out towers and the pointed turrets.

Working with Tommy turned out to be much easier than working with her group at school. Her classmates all had their own ideas, and it took ages to agree on the smallest detail. But Tommy worked quietly, willing to follow any of Karen's suggestions. When one of her plans didn't work out he didn't tease her. He simply flattened the mess, and they started all over again.

One of Karen's best ideas was to dig a moat. A moat, she explained to Tommy, was a kind of ditch filled with water. "We'll dig the moat all around our castle. Then at the very end of the contest we'll fill it with water," she said, "and it will look incredible."

One morning Karen asked Grandma for a drive to the town beach so that she and Tommy could practice.

"Now, Karen," warned Grandma, "you're not starting to take this too seriously, are you? It's supposed to be fun."

"Sure thing, Grandma. But it will be even more fun if we win!" And even while Grandma was shaking her head they had piled into the back seat of the car.

As they drove, Tommy sat next to her, silent as usual. Karen reflected that she missed having someone her own age to talk to.

Then in no time at all, it was the weekend.

"Well, my sweet," said Grandma at breakfast, "Grandpa will be coming up from the city this afternoon. When I spoke to him last night he said he might bring a surprise."

"A surprise?" Karen was wide-eyed. "What kind of surprise?"

"Well, if I told you it wouldn't be a surprise, would it? You'll just have to wait and see. By the way, Martin Cooper's coming over this morning. He's promised to pick up the blueberry pies for the barbecue tomorrow."

"Marty's coming? Maybe I'll wear my new shorts," said Karen thoughtfully and then she raced to the bedroom.

Grandma laughed. She knew her granddaughter had a crush on Martin Cooper. Ever since Karen could remember, Martin had been captain of the summer baseball team. Although he was at university now and working in the city during the summer, he often came to the lake on weekends.

It was Martin who assigned every player a position. Two summers ago, when Karen was only eight, it was Martin who showed her how to shorten her hold on the bat and bunt the ball. To Karen's delight she had made a base hit right away – even now she could hear the crack! of the bat as the ball flew out over the field.

"Well, if it isn't the city slugger," exclaimed

Martin, slamming the car door behind him. "Here, let me take a look at you. You know, you've grown a lot since last year. Maybe you'll be our power hitter this year!"

"No way," Karen protested, "I want to do something I'm good at, and I know I can bunt."

"You sure can. But the All-Stars also know it. Sometimes it's good to change your strategy, keep the other side guessing."

"Then let them think I'm going to do something different, and I'll surprise them by doing the same thing."

Karen wasn't going to admit that she was afraid to try something new. What if she couldn't hit the ball at all? Karen hated being teased.

"OK. You do whatever feels right." Karen could tell that Martin still wished she'd just try. Then he changed the subject. "Say, I was sorry to hear about Michael. How's he coming along?"

"Fine, I guess. But breaking his ankle didn't change things at all. He's still a brat."

"C'mon, Karen. Be nice. He's just a little kid. And speaking of kids – wait till you see what I've got for our team." Martin pulled a large package from the front seat of his car.

"You know I'm working for a T-shirt manufacturer this summer? Well, my boss let me design these." He held out a white T-shirt with a sketch of three goats wearing baseball caps. Below the goats were the words "Summer Kids."

Karen began to laugh. "Oh, Marty, are you ever weird. Summer Kids. That's a riot!" Grinning, Martin passed her the T-shirt. Karen held it up for size – her new shorts showed underneath.

"Your grandmother told me there's another kid renting your cottage," said Martin. "We'll have to get him on the team."

"Tommy? He's really small. I don't think he's much of a ballplayer."

"Never you mind about that. We have enough players to balance one or two weak ones."

And then Martin went into the kitchen to collect the blueberry pies. Karen helped load them into the trunk, and she waved goodbye as he drove off. The morning was almost over.

After lunch Grandma said she had to go into town for a few things, so Karen went too. When they got back, Grandpa's blue car was parked in the driveway.

"Grandpa, you're here!" shouted Karen as she ran up to the porch. "Did you have a good week at the office? Where's the surprise?"

Grandpa met her with his finger to his lips. "Shhh," he whispered. "Talk quietly or you'll wake up the surprise."

"Wake up the surprise?" repeated Karen in a whisper. "What kind of surprise is this?"

"Your mother – she came up for the weekend." Karen peeked behind Grandpa as he headed out the door. There, stretched out on the couch, was Karen's mom, fast asleep. Karen tiptoed over to her, kissed her gently on the forehead, and then tiptoed outside again. She found Grandma and Grandpa, down at the dock.

Grandpa explained to Karen that her mom was frazzled from staying home with Michael every day. So her dad had offered to take over for the weekend.

"She wanted to surprise you! But you weren't here when we drove up, and the couch looked so lonely without someone lying on it," he concluded, laughing.

While they were catching up on the news Karen's mom appeared at the dock.

"So here you are," she said, with a sleepy smile. "I thought you'd abandoned me."

After kisses and hellos all around, Grandma said she was going to make some iced tea. Grandpa wanted to change into his shorts.

Mom sat down beside Karen. "Well," she said. "Let me look at my little pumpkin. You haven't changed much. I'd still recognize you in a crowd."

"Mom," Karen groaned, "I haven't been away that long."

"It seems as if you've been away for a month."

"Michael?"

Mom sighed. "His ankle is healing beautifully, according to Dr. Josephs. But he's so cranky and crabby. First, he wants me to read a story. But he doesn't want any of the books we've got in the house. Then he wants me to play a game with him, and after two turns he loses interest. Even having a friend over doesn't work. They end up arguing."

Karen nodded her head sympathetically. He was usually like that, she thought.

"Anyway," Mom went on, "your perceptive

father decided that we needed a break from each other for a couple of days, and so here I am." She stretched out in the sunlight.

"Hmmm," she murmured, "this feels good. I don't think I'll get too many wrinkles if I sit here for a few minutes. Tell me what you did this week, Pumpkin."

Karen told her about the trips to town with Grandma, about picking blueberries, about the books she'd read. Finally she told her about Tommy, Dawn, and the sandcastle contest.

"Mom, I need your advice."

Karen's mom put up her hand, stop-sign fashion. "Hold it! I forgot to warn you that I am not acting in my motherly capacity this weekend."

"What?"

"A holiday is a holiday. This weekend I am my mother's daughter. If you need a parent, go ask Grandma or Grandpa."

"Oh, Mother. Well, can I ask your advice as a friend?"

"All right." Mom let out a sigh. "I knew my shoulders couldn't stay weightless for long. What is it?"

"It's Tommy, Mom. He's ... well, he's kind of strange."

"What do you mean?"

"I don't know. That's part of the problem. He's like Michael in some ways, but mostly not like him at all."

"Why should he be? No two kids are the same, Karen."

"I know, but that's not what I mean. For one thing, Tommy talks funny, like a baby."

"Not every child is as articulate as your brother."

Karen snorted, "Right. No wonder Dad calls him motor mouth! But that's what I don't understand. Tommy talks like a baby, but he draws and writes so well, not just printing, you know, and you should see what he built with his Lego set. It's incredible!"

"Well, different children have different skills, Karen. But I'll see what I can find out."

Karen protested. "That's what Grandma said she'd do."

"And?" asked Mom.

"Nothing," reported Karen. "She's never said

anything about him to me."

"Perhaps there's nothing to tell about Tommy."

Karen clenched her teeth. She was convinced there had to be some explanation for Tommy's strangeness. And she would keep trying to find out what it was.

7

SUNDAY MORNING dawned hot and hazy. "Good thing it's so humid," Karen told Tommy. "Maybe the sand won't dry out so fast, and our castle will hold together longer."

She was eager to get to the beach on time, so Karen kept hurrying everyone along. "Okay, already," complained Mom in a good-natured way. "Don't rush me; I'm on holiday."

At the beach they learned that only six teams had registered. "The fewer the teams, the better your chances," pointed out Grandpa, winking at Tommy.

Karen checked out the competition. Except for the four Campbell sisters, who would also play in the baseball game that afternoon, Karen didn't know anyone. The lifeguards organizing the contest had placed a small cardboard sign for each team in a different site on the beach. Karen was pleased to find the sign for the Burton team at the far end of the beach. Great, she thought, we won't be disturbed by other people.

The lifeguards called the teams together and read the rules aloud. Each team had fifteen minutes to build one castle; team members must work together; only materials found on the beach would be acceptable: sand, pebbles, sticks, and found objects.

One of the lifeguards blew her whistle, and the contest began. While Karen filled the pails with damp sand from the water's edge, Tommy began to dig a ditch around their site. Then Karen lined the ditch with small stones while Tommy emptied the first pails of sand.

It was exciting! Karen couldn't tear her eyes away from their castle. But in the distance she heard voices arguing – one of the Campbells had overturned a pail of sand on her sister's foot.

It began to look as if the hours of practice were going to pay off. The Burton castle was rising steadily from the sand. Karen was shaping the look-out towers and the rounded turrets; Tommy was connecting the towers with walls and ramps.

Just before the lifeguard put the whistle to her lips, Karen hastily filled her pail with water. Floating in the foam was a bright pink plastic object. She grabbed it, raced back and stuck it into the highest tower just as the blast of the whistle cut through the air.

Karen and Tommy stood nervously beside their castle while the judges worked their way down the beach. A small crowd followed, including Grandma, Grandpa, Mom, and Dawn. Finally, they arrived in front of the Burton castle.

Karen poured her pail of water into the stone-lined moat. The stones held the water for a few moments before it slowly drained into the sand.

"Now *that's* a castle," said one judge, the town librarian.

"That not a castle, that a fort," corrected Tommy.

Karen stepped on Tommy's foot. "Actually, this is a fortress," she announced loudly. "You can see how this moat protects the castle from enemies."

The librarian seemed to be looking at the pink

object stuck in the tower. "And this is the king's flag," explained Karen, "because he happens to be in residence right now."

The librarian turned to speak to the other two judges. Karen adjusted the "flag", the small pink pennant stamped with the words "Dairy Dell" that she had found in the water.

Then the judges turned to face the crowd. "Well," said the librarian, "we think the Burton team has put together the most creative presentation on the beach today. We hereby proclaim you King and Queen of the Castle." Everyone clapped loudly; Grandpa cheered. Another judge pinned shiny gold ribbons on Karen and Tommy.

Tommy tugged at his ribbon. "What this?" he asked Karen.

"It means we won First Prize," Karen whispered.

Tommy's face broke into a smile. "WE winned! You mean WE winned?" He began to jump up and down. His face was flushed with excitement. His eyes were sparkling. Karen had never seen him so happy.

Then the third judge presented Karen and

Tommy with gift certificates from the local toy-store. They knelt proudly beside their castle while a photographer from the community paper took their photograph. Lots of people came over to shake their hands. "I winned," Tommy told every-one. "See I winned!"

He was making such a fuss that Karen was embarrassed. Whenever she had imagined how they would behave if they won the contest, Tommy would be silent, as usual, and she would be modest and cool. She would wave off praise with an "Oh-it-was-nothing" shrug.

Now here was Tommy jumping up and down with joy, while she stood silently nearby. As she turned to look at the castle Karen saw how much of the work had been Tommy's. With a start, she also realized how much all of this meant to Tommy. Maybe I had the idea, she thought, but I never believed he would take it so seriously. Sud-denly Karen felt guilty – had she used Tommy?

"Take me home, Mommy," she pleaded.

"What's the matter, Pumpkin? Sudden fame too much for you?"

Karen shook her head.

"Don't you want to see who wins the other prizes?" asked Mom.

Karen shook her head again. "I just want to go home."

"Alrighty," said Mom. "Let's see if we can find your grandparents."

8

AS KAREN AND HER MOTHER walked to the lake for a swim after the morning's excitement, Mom remarked, "You know, Karen, your intuition was right. There is something different about Tommy."

"What?"

"Well, the reason that he talks so funny, as you put it, is that he has a severe language delay."

Karen stopped walking. Her eyes opened wide. "See? I told you! I knew there was something wrong. No one wanted to believe me. But I knew I was right." Karen suddenly stopped.

"How did you find out?" she demanded.

"Dawn told me as we were walking on the beach this morning," Mom replied.

"Does Grandma know about this too?"

"I guess so."

"Why didn't Grandma tell me? I told her I thought Tommy was strange."

"I don't think Grandma knew about Tommy at first," said Mom. "But when you asked her questions, she began to wonder. Then I guess she spoke to Dawn. By that time you and Tommy were involved with this sandcastle project. I suppose they decided you two were such good friends that there was no point in telling you."

"Friends!" Karen couldn't believe her ears. "Tommy is NOT my friend! He's just a summer kid. It so happened there was nobody else around." Karen was steaming. "If I had known about his language problem, if someone had told me, maybe I could have helped him."

"You're right. Maybe people should walk around with labels on their foreheads. Your label would say, 'I like to read, but can't hit a baseball.' Tommy's label would say, 'I have a language delay.' "

"But he can draw and build very well," Karen added.

"His forehead is too small for two sentences," Mom countered. Karen allowed a small smile.

"No, I don't think labels are a good idea," Mom concluded.

Karen's smile faded. A frown creased her forehead. "Say, Mom, just what is a language delay?"

"It means that he hasn't learned to talk at the same rate as other children. He goes to a special class to help him. Anyway, that's enough talking for now. I think you should ask Dawn about this. Right now, let's swim." And she dove into the lake.

Easy for Mom, thought Karen. She isn't stuck having to play with a kid with a severe language delay, whatever that is. True, some of Michael's friends still didn't speak that clearly. Did lots of six-year olds speak like that? Did they all have language delays? Would they have to go to a special class? There was so much she'd have to ask Dawn about later.

Karen sighed. She might as well go swimming, she decided, and put Tommy out of her mind. After all, he was just a summer kid. That reminded her about the baseball game in the afternoon. One more thing to do with Tommy. But he was leaving tomorrow and she'd probably never have to see him again.

9

"IT'S TOO HOT to play baseball," grumbled Karen.

"But this game is just for fun," said Grandpa, parking the car behind the school. "You play the best you can, and we'll all have a grand time. Besides, you're on a roll – maybe you'll hit a home run this afternoon."

Martin Cooper was already handing out T-shirts when they arrived.

"Say, champ," he called when he saw Karen. "I hear you're a Master Builder. I didn't know you were so talented. Congratulations!"

"Oh, you should really congratulate Tommy." Karen was embarrassed. "He's the Master Builder. I just helped with the design."

"You're too modest, Karen. But where is Tommy, anyway?"

Even as Martin asked the question Tommy appeared with his mother. Martin shook Tommy's hand, offered his congratulations, and handed him a T-shirt.

"I hope we're not late," apologized Dawn. "It took me a while to convince Tommy that he should wear his baseball cap. It's such a hot sun today."

"Absolutely," agreed Martin. "Can't play baseball without a baseball cap." And he smiled at Tommy, who stared back without expression.

Dawn helped Tommy pull the T-shirt over his head. The hero of the morning at the beach was suddenly swallowed up in the oversize shirt. With his baseball cap wobbling over his ears, it was as if Tommy had shrunk to his earlier, timid self.

Everyone loved the T-shirts. "Cute," said Patricia, the eldest Campbell. This year she was assigned to centrefield. "Don't send any balls my way," she warned Paul Greco, the pitcher.

Paul and Mauro, the Greco twins, were twelve this year. Karen could never tell them apart. Paul always pitched for the team and Mauro was usually shortstop.

This year the All-Stars were first at bat, so

Martin spread out his team over the field.

"Okay, Karen, you take your usual place in right field; Tommy can give you a hand." Martin put himself in left field, leaving Patricia to hold the centre.

The game began. The first All-Star batter hit two foul balls behind the batting cage and then made a base hit. Paul walked the next hitter.

"What happened?" teased Mauro.

"I'm still warming up," retorted Paul.

The third batter managed to get another base hit, but a quick throw from Mauro put the runner out on second. There were All-Stars on first and third bases when the kid known as "Slugger" came up to bat. Karen didn't know her real name. Last year "Slugger" hit a spectacular home run with all bases loaded.

The All-Stars were beginning to gloat. "Here comes our first three runs," one of them boasted.

Paul pulled his cap down over his eyes, rubbed his right hand on the seat of his pants, and threw his speediest ball. But "Slugger" sent it bouncing back over the grass in Karen's direction, and took off for first base.

"Go for it, Karen!" yelled Martin.

Karen raced to meet the ball. As she ran she extended her glove, ready to meet the ball as it bounced toward her. Just as the ball came thundering down, she felt Tommy tug at her T-shirt. "Look, Karen." He was excited. "I see buttercups. Come look."

It was just enough to break her concentration, and the ball skidded under her arm to fly further down the field.

"Don't bother, I've got it," called Patricia. A burst of cheering from the stand told Karen that the first runner had made it to home base.

Patricia scooped up the ball, and lobbed it over to Martin, as another cheer went up at home plate – the second runner was home free. Martin threw smoothly to third base, just in time to pin down "Slugger".

Karen trudged over to Martin, her head low. "I'm sorry," she told him.

"Don't let it worry you," he assured her. "We'll make up for it when it's our turn at bat."

"Good try, Pumpkin!" Karen heard her Mom yelling from the stands, where she was sitting with

Dawn. Karen could see the bright buttercups Dawn was holding in one hand as she gestured to Tommy with the other – she was pointing him back to the field.

"Let him stay with you," Karen muttered to herself. "Some help he is."

The game resumed. The next batter struck out, and the one following hit a slow pop fly swiftly squelched by Paul. The score was still 2–0 for the All-Stars.

And now the Summer Kids were at bat. Martin always set the line-up according to age, youngest first. That way, he explained, the little ones got up quickly without getting too impatient, and the older ones, who usually had more power, could start hitting when the game got really exciting.

He was checking the ages of his players. Tommy stood up tall when his turn came. "I be ten soon," he announced.

"Huh?" blurted Karen in disbelief. "That's impossible. He can't be anywhere near ten. I'll go check with Dawn."

"Sure," agreed Martin.

"Soon I be ten," insisted Tommy.

Karen sprinted over to Dawn. "Dawn, how old is Tommy? He says he's almost ten."

"Well sort of. His birthday's at the end of November."

Karen's jaw dropped. Tommy almost ten? Impossible. He didn't look – or act – like an almost-ten-year-old. Was this for real?

"C'mon, Karen," called Martin. "You're holding up the game."

"Is something wrong?" Dawn asked Karen.

"N-n-no," said Karen. She walked slowly back to the team, trying to make sense of this new information.

"Well?" asked Martin.

"He'll be ten in November," Karen reported, shaking her head.

"Hmmm," said Martin, "then we'll let him bat just before you. Okay, everybody line up, and good luck."

The Summer Kids led off with somebody's visiting grandson. He was so eager to swing the bat that he swung as soon as the ball had left the pitcher's glove, a wild miss. He did this twice more. "Out," ruled the umpire.

Next up was the youngest Campbell, Tracy. Martin had taught her to bunt, too, and she sent the ball flying between the pitcher's legs. Off she scooted to first base.

"Good hit, Tracy," called Martin.

"Three cheers for the Campbells, " yelled her sister.

Next up was Tommy.

"Okay, Tommy," coached Martin. "You do what Tracy did. Hit it low and bouncy. Make them scramble for it."

"I hit a pop fly," said Tommy. "My ball go straight up."

"OK, you just do the best you can."

The first pitch whizzed by. Tommy swung after the catcher had already caught the ball.

"Come on, baby," called out Mauro. "Smack that ball." Tommy slammed the bat to the ground. "I not a baby! I be Thomas!" he yelled. And he ran over to Mauro, to pound him in the chest.

"Hey, take it easy," protested Mauro. "I was just trying to be friendly."

Tommy was still pounding him with both fists. "I be Thomas," he shouted again. "I be the King of the Castle."

Laughing, Mauro began to sing the old taunt: "I'm the King of the Castle, and you're a little rascal."

Tommy's eyes were wet, but he kept punching. "I no baby," he screamed.

By this time Martin was holding both of Tommy's arms. "It's okay, Tommy, no one's calling you a baby. That's just a way of talking." He looked over Tommy's head to Karen.

And for Karen it was as if the pieces of a puzzle had finally slipped into place. Suddenly the word "delay" made sense to her; to be delayed, to be late. Tommy's ability to understand and to speak were delayed; it was late in happening, so late that he was an almost-ten-year-old who didn't even speak as well as a six-year-old.

But that was hardly his fault. Karen found herself shouting, "He doesn't understand! He doesn't know what you're saying." She glared at all of them. "Leave him alone. Tommy is my friend, and you leave him alone." And then she knew she was going to cry. She pushed her way past the crowd, away from the game.

"So, who started this anyway?" protested Mauro. "Calm down."

"Calm down," repeated Tommy scornfully. He gave Mauro one last push. "You make my friend Karen sad." Then he ran off after her.

"I sorry," Tommy said when he caught up. "I no fight no more."

"Oh, Tommy," said Karen. "I'm so sorry that you get into fights because you don't understand what people mean. Mauro didn't mean that you're a baby. 'Come on baby' is just an expression. He really wanted you to hit the ball."

"Oh? I no fight no more."

"Well sometimes you might have to fight. Only it's better to use words, than your fists." But even as she said it, Karen knew this would be hard to explain. Maybe when he's older, she thought.

The second inning had started by the time Dawn found them sitting quietly on the front steps of the school. She put her arm across Tommy's shoulders. "I'm glad you're feeling better. Would you like to get a drink before going back to the game?" Then she turned to Karen as Tommy started off. "Karen, I don't know what to say to you. I feel so terrible that this happened."

"Yeah," Karen shrugged. "How was I supposed to understand when no one told me anything?"

"I wanted to. There were a couple of times I almost did."

"Then why didn't you?" Anger swirled in Karen. "I knew there was something wrong from the minute I saw him. I thought he was strange, weird."

Dawn sighed, "I know, I know. But that's part of the problem. Even after people know the truth they still treat him as if he's weird."

"How?"

"Sometimes," Dawn explained, "they treat Tommy as if he's deaf, so they shout or talk loudly. Sometimes they get the idea that he doesn't understand, so they talk baby talk to him. But that doesn't help – how is he to learn to speak like the rest of us unless he hears us talk?"

"Is that why you never let Tommy out of your sight?" Karen asked.

Dawn smiled, "I guess I have to learn to give him a bit more independence. But it's so hard. I've been fighting on his behalf for such a long time now – first, to find out what his problem was, then to get him into a special class at school."

"You could have trusted me. I would have understood."

"I didn't want to take the chance. Besides, you two got along so well, I thought I didn't have to."

"Got along well?" Karen's anger came back. "I didn't want to have anything to do with him."

"But you got him involved in the sandcastle contest."

"That was to give me something to do. He just happened to be around."

"Doesn't matter," Dawn smiled again. "You didn't put him down or call him names, you just treated him like a regular kid."

"No, I didn't. I treated him like he was six years old, like my little brother."

"That's what I mean," Dawn repeated. "You treated him like a regular kid."

*

A few hours later, Karen joined a group of the

Summer Kids at the barbecue. Everyone wanted to talk about the ball game – next year they were sure would be different, each of them would play better. But Karen soon lost interest in talking about baseball.

She looked around for Tommy. It took her a few minutes to search through the crowd at the Coopers' cottage. Finally she found him standing at the dock, alone. He was tossing stones listlessly into the water.

Karen watched him for a moment, and then walked down to the water's edge and picked up a stone. She aimed carefully, and threw it lightly across the surface of the lake. It skipped across and entered with a soft splash near the spot where Tommy's stone had plopped in a moment before. Tommy turned to Karen. He smiled up at her, and aimed carefully as she had done. Then, just like Karen, he sent his stone skimming across the water in three graceful skips.

EPILOGUE

KAREN LIKED her Grade Five class. Ms Miller's room had two computers, which meant twice as much time at the keyboard for Karen.

Michael's ankle seemed to have mended. As far as Karen could tell from the noise he made as he chased his friends around the yard, he wasn't hurting too badly.

September was good – Karen always loved the beginning of the year, seeing her friends again and starting new routines. And October was fun, especially getting ready for Halloween. But in November the whole world seemed to grow dull and dreary. Even the clouds, heavy with winter weather, sagged in the colourless sky.

It was on such a grey November day that Karen came home from school to find a letter waiting for her.

The handwriting was unusually neat ...

Dear Karen,
    How are you?
    I am fine.
    I go to school. I like it. My class has five boys and three girls.
    I remember at the cottage. My mother say maybe we go back there this summer. Will you go at the cottage too?

                    Your friend,
                    Thomas Jones

P. S. I eat blueberry pie now. It taste good.

There was another sheet of paper folded in the envelope. Tommy had drawn a picture of the sand-castle with the pink plastic pennant in one of the towers and water swirling in the moat. He had drawn himself and Karen standing next to the castle wearing their ribbons.

Karen looked at the picture for a moment, smiled, and walked into the kitchen to put it on the refrigerator door.

THE END

MYRNA NEURINGER LEVY

Myrna Neuringer Levy loves to work
with young people, and has been a
teacher and a librarian for many years.
The Summer Kid is her first book.